There and back again

This book is due for return on or before the last date indicated
on label. Renewals may be obtained on application.

PERTH AND KINROSS DISTRICT LIBRARIES

THERE & BACK AGAIN

HAROLD JONES

LITTLE GREATS

RANDOM HOUSE

LONDON SYDNEY
AUCKLAND JOHANNESBURG

Bunby felt cross and lonely. Richard and Lucy had gone
out for the day and left him behind.

Suddenly
he had an idea.
He would go
out in Richard's
sailing boat.

He went down to
the kitchen and
made himself some
sandwiches for
his lunch.

But when he was ready to set off he found he could not
carry the boat to the stream on his own.

He asked the dog to help him but the dog was too lazy.
Then the Siamese cat came into the room.

She and Bunby carried the boat to the stream.

"Goodbye," said Bunby.

Soon he was sailing quickly down the stream past all kinds of animals, who looked at him in surprise.

It was the first time Bunby had been out alone. He felt very brave and very excited.

Suddenly a great gust of wind blew the boat into the reeds.

Bunby was thrown into the water. He couldn't swim!

He might have drowned. Two swans pulled him out just in time.

But they couldn't save his sandwiches.

Bunby thanked them and they swam away. But how was
he going to get home? His boat was stuck in the reeds.

Sadly Bunby took off his wet clothes and hung them up
to dry. He lay down in the sun and soon fell asleep.

Then he woke up with a jump. A pigeon was standing in front of him. "Oh!" said Bunby, "my boat is stuck in the reeds and I don't know the way home." "Don't worry," said the pigeon, "you can fly home on my back. But why don't you come and see my friends in the forest first. It isn't far away."

So away they flew, high above the countryside, over fields and farms.

The pigeon landed in a glade in the forest. Bunby was thirsty.

He leaned over and drank from a little stream.

When he looked up, the forest

was full of animals!

They had all come to meet him. The squirrels brought him

leaves and berries to eat because he had lost his sandwiches.

And the owl entertained them

with a ghost story.

Then it was time to go.

Bunby came home just before Richard and Lucy. The cat and the dog were waiting anxiously for him by the door.

They thought he had got lost.

When Richard and Lucy returned, Bunby was sitting there
as if he had never been away.

The next day Mr. Jones called round with Richard's boat.
He had found it in the stream a long way from their garden.
Richard and Lucy couldn't think how it had got there.
And Bunby never said a word.

For Laura

First published in Great Britain 1977 by
Oxford University Press
First published in *Little Greats* edition 1993
by Julia MacRae for Random House
20 Vauxhall Bridge Road, London SW1V 2SA
Random House Australia (Pty) Ltd
20 Alfred Street, Milsons Point, Sydney, NSW 2061
Random House New Zealand Ltd
18 Poland Road, Glenfield, Auckland, New Zealand
Random House, South Africa (Pty) Ltd
PO Box 337, Bergvlei, 2012, South Africa
Printed in Hong Kong
British Library Cataloguing-in-Publication Data
A catalogue record for this book is available
from the British Library
ISBN 1-85681-068-2